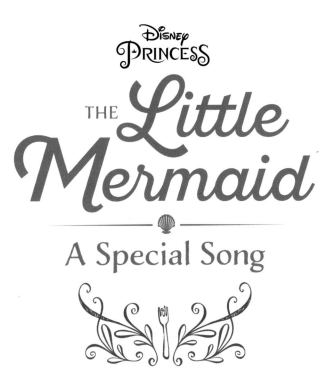

Disney PRINCESS

THE Little Mermaid

A Special Song

Written by
Lisa Ann Marsoli

Illustrated by the
Disney Storybook Art Team

This book belongs to:

_____

DISNEY PRINCESS

THE Little Mermaid

A Special Song

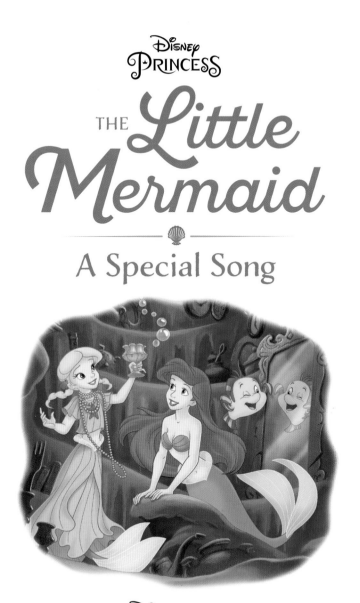

DISNEY PRESS

Los Angeles • New York

Originally published by Disney Press © 2005 Disney Enterprises, Inc.

For information address Disney Press, 1200 Grand Central Avenue,
Glendale, California 91201.

ISBN 978-1-368-02804-2
FAC-023680-18211
Printed in China
First Box Set Edition, July 2018
1 3 5 7 9 10 8 6 4 2

For more Disney Press fun, visit www.disneybooks.com
This book was printed on paper created from a sustainable source.

"May I have your attention, please?" Sebastian the crab called.

The crab tapped his baton on a podium. King Triton's birthday was in a couple of days, and the court musicians were planning a special performance. Triton's daughter, Ariel, would sing while the orchestra played a brand-new tune. Sebastian wanted the concert to be spectacular, but they still had a lot of work to do.

The crab raised his baton, and the musicians began to play. Beautiful music filled the sea, until—*clang!*

"Who did that?" Sebastian demanded.

"Um . . . I did," a young mermaid named Coral replied quietly.

"The best way to play the cymbals is to hold on to them! Now, if there are no more interruptions," Sebastian said grumpily, "let's continue."

The rehearsal went from bad to worse. Coral dropped her cymbal a second time. *Clang!* Then she tripped and landed on top of a kettledrum.

As Ariel watched, Sebastian threw down his baton. "Rehearsal is over!" the crab yelled and stormed off.

Ariel helped Coral up. "Don't mind Sebastian."

"I'll never be able to get this song right—let alone perfect!" Coral said sadly.

"Don't worry about it," Ariel said. "The only thing *I'm* perfect at is making Sebastian mad. You should have seen his face the last time I went to the surface."

"You've been to the surface?" Coral asked, amazed. "You must be the bravest mermaid ever!"

"It's just something I like to do," Ariel said. "I'm always gathering treasures. Would you like to see my collection?"

"I'd love to!" Coral exclaimed.

The two mermaids swam to Ariel's grotto.

"Make yourself at home," Ariel told Coral when they arrived. Flounder the fish was there. He waved a fin at them.

The young mermaid swam around, examining jewelry and shiny trinkets. "Where did you find all of this?" Coral asked as she put on a strand of pearls.

"I found some of it in sunken ships," replied Ariel.

"You've been inside a sunken ship?" Coral said with a gasp. "Weren't you scared?"

"Of course not. Were you, Flounder?" Ariel teased.

"Nothing to it!" the fish fibbed.

"So what are we waiting for?" Ariel asked. "Let's go!"

Coral and Flounder trailed behind Ariel. Soon they arrived at a ship that had sunk to the ocean floor.

"Let's see what's in there!" Ariel urged.

Her friends followed her through a large porthole.

Inside the ship, Ariel found an old steamer trunk. "Look at this!" she cried, holding up a purple parasol.

"And this!" Coral exclaimed, picking up a fancy lampshade. "I wonder what it's for?"

"My friend Scuttle can tell us," Ariel said. "Follow me!"

"Where are we going?" Coral asked Flounder.

"To the surface," he replied matter-of-factly.

Soon the friends arrived at the surface. Scuttle the seagull examined their treasures. "That is a *twirleriffer*!" he said, looking at Coral's lampshade. "It's what humans wear when they're going somewhere important."

Before long, the friends had to leave.

As they headed home, Coral asked Ariel if she could keep the *twirleriffer* at the grotto. "It might get broken at home," she explained.

"Of course," Ariel agreed. "The grotto is my secret place, and it can be yours, too."

A few days later, as Ariel swam toward the grotto, she heard someone singing. The voice was strong and clear—but sweet, too.

When Ariel arrived, she saw her new friend.

"Coral! I didn't know you had such a lovely voice! You should be singing in the concert, not playing the cymbals."

The little blond mermaid shrugged. "I just like singing to myself," she explained. "I've never actually performed."

The next day at rehearsal, Sebastian made Ariel
and the orchestra practice over and over, but something
always seemed to go wrong.

"The big day is tomorrow!" the crab said, fretting. "This
concert needs to be fit for a king—King Triton, to be exact!
Let's try it again." So they did. The rehearsal went on and on.

By the end of the afternoon, everyone was tired.

"See you tomorrow," Ariel said. Her voice was raspy.

On the day of the concert, Ariel could only whisper. She had lost her voice! Luckily, she knew who could take her place.

"Me?" Coral said when the princess asked her. "But I can't!"

"You must!" Sebastian insisted. "Otherwise King Triton's birthday celebration will be ruined!"

"I can't sing in front of a crowd of merpeople," Coral said, pleading.

"Sure you can," Flounder said.

Coral thought about how she had visited a sunken ship and gone to the surface, things she had never thought she could do—all because of Ariel. Now her new friend was counting on her.

"All right," Coral said slowly. "I'll do it."

That night, when Coral peeked out from backstage, she nearly fainted. The entire kingdom was there—including her parents and her brothers and sisters! King Triton and Ariel sat in the royal box.

When it was time, Coral took a deep breath and swam onstage. As the orchestra started playing, she sang softly. But as she went on, Coral's voice got louder. Before she knew it, the concert was over, and the audience began to clap and cheer.

"Coral," said Sebastian, smiling, "you can give away your cymbals. From now on, you're going to be a court singer!"

After the show, Ariel went to congratulate her friend.
She found Coral with her family.

"I didn't know you could sing like that!" one of Coral's
sisters exclaimed.

"No one ever would have known if it wasn't for Ariel,"
replied Coral. "She believed in me."

Ariel still couldn't speak, but she gave Coral a big hug.
It had been a wonderful evening.